GODZILLA™
JOURNEY TO MONSTER ISLAND

by Scott Ciencin
illustrated by Bob Eggleton

Random House New York

Cover art and interior illustrations by Bob Eggleton.
Text and art copyright © 1998 Toho Co., Ltd.
Godzilla, Godzillasaurus, Anguirus, Kamacuras,
Kumonga, Rodan, Varan, and the character designs
are trademarks of Toho Co., Ltd.

http://www.randomhouse.com/

Library of Congress Catalog Card Number: 97-75902
ISBN: 0-679-88901-9
RL: 4.5

Printed in the United States of America 10 9 8 7 6 5 4 3 2 1

PROLOGU

*Zigong, central China
170 million years ago*

The Godzillasaurus plung
through the lowland for
With his wildly swinging
he shattered the trunks of th
conifer trees. His every footfall made the gro
tremble.

A club-tailed Shunosaurus wandered into his p
and gave a cry of alarm. At forty feet long, the c
tail was no match for the larger predator, an
quickly moved out of the way.

Ignoring the club-tail, the Godzillasaurus contir
forward, on the trail of something bigger. Whe
caught a glimpse of green and golden scales flas
in the sunlight up ahead, he roared in triumph.
sound made his prey shudder and hesitate.

The Godzillasaurus closed the gap separating
m from the other dinosaur. His prey was in a
lind panic. He watched as it stumbled over a fallen
ee and landed on its side, shaking the ground.

With a bone-chilling cry, the triumphant Godzillasaurus came within inches of his prey—and
leaped past him. The fallen dinosaur, another Godzillasaurus, bellowed with rage. But the victor in the
race ignored him.

Five hundred yards ahead lay the clearing that
marked the finish of the race. The running
Godzillasaurus covered the distance before his
opponent could get to his feet.

With a holler of pure delight, the first Godzillasaurus burst into the clearing and hurled himself
into the cool, refreshing water of a winding river.
He struck hard and the water rose up around him,
splashing an entire clan of spike-backs on the
stream's far side.

The Godzillasaurus rolled onto his back, letting
the warm sun bake his belly. What a fun game!

His fellow Godzillasaurus limped defeatedly from
the edge of the clearing. He came to the bank and
dunked his head in the water.

A crimson-winged pterosaur flew overhead. The
Godzillasaurus and his companion watched as the
creature arced down and skimmed the far surface
of the stream with its beak.

The pterosaur's large curved teeth reached from its maw like curling claws. Its head was a blur as it plunged into the water and snatched a fish. Content, the pterosaur took to the skies.

The pterosaur was a little thing, its wingspan no more than five feet. But it was very pretty for the Godzillasaurus to watch.

A sharp *crack* snagged his attention. He turned his head to find a pair of stegosaurs locking horns. The Godzillasaurus knew this game. The last one to remain on the shore won. The *crack* sounded again, and one of the stegosaurs fell into the water.

The Godzillasaurus's companion nudged him with his tail. He looked up and saw the head of a plant-eater descending toward him, a huge collection of leaves hanging from her mouth. She brushed the leaves against the Godzillasaurus's scaly face. The Godzillasaurus writhed happily, splashing his companion. It tickled!

Leaning back in the warm sunshine, the Godzillasaurus wished this could go on forever. But it couldn't—it was only a dream.

And with that sudden, shocking understanding, the dreamer woke.

CHAPTER

I

South central Washington
The present

"Amy, come on! The storm's getting worse. It's not safe here!"

Twelve-year-old Amy O'Neil woke suddenly. The cold chill hit her hard. She tugged her oversized flannel shirt more tightly around her. She was freezing! Even the turtleneck she wore underneath didn't help.

Her twin brother, Roy, was crouching over her. His face was wet, his hair soaked. As usual, he was frowning. The grim expression marred his otherwise handsome face—blue eyes, high cheekbones, soft brown hair that was desperately in need of a trim.

His clothes were a little baggy, too—and about two years out of fashion. Of course, that wasn't his fault. He hadn't picked them out.

4

Thunder interrupted Amy's thoughts. She looked around. The night's black sky had lightened to a gray dawn, and a downpour of rain was beginning.

"But I was so warm," Amy muttered. "And it all seemed so real..."

Amy felt a tingling sensation inside her head. Then she heard her brother's voice in her mind. *Get over it. You were dreaming. Duh.*

Cut that out! she shot back with her own thoughts. She didn't like it when Roy used the special bond they shared just to dis her. Reading minds was a powerful thing, and thoughts were often more intense than speech.

Lightning struck a cliff a hundred yards away. The blinding flash charged the air with electricity. Amy pulled her flannel shirt tight again, then got to her feet and looked around. She and Roy had spent the night on the side of this mountain, cradled behind a group of large boulders.

Roy pointed at a winding trail. "That'll take us to higher ground."

"Yeah, but the lightning—"

"There are caves. Protection. We need to reach them."

Amy nodded. Roy started along the rocky trail, and she followed. After a few minutes, Roy shifted the weight of the bag he carried. In the bag was a flashlight, some food, and some other supplies he'd "borrowed" from the orphanage.

"I can't believe we left Crestview for this crazy rescue attempt," Roy complained.

"It's not crazy. And it's not my fault none of the grownups would listen to me when they were putting together the search parties. I used to tutor Billy in math. I told you, he—"

"I know, I know. He used to daydream about coming out here to the mountains. And sometimes you listened in on his thoughts."

"I had to check whether he was paying attention, didn't I?" Amy pointed out. "But yeah. He'd pretend there were dragons here. Whole families of them. And one day they'd adopt him."

Roy frowned. "Poor kid. Just couldn't cope with living at the orphanage, I guess."

Amy didn't like the sound of that at all. She recalled an image from Billy's daydreams and sent it roaring into her twin brother's thoughts.

Suddenly, Roy's mind received the vision of a huge green-scaled dragon speaking with Amy's voice: *It's no crime, having an imagination! You should try it sometime.*

"Hey!" Roy cried, swatting at the air in front of him as if the fire-breather were really there.

Amy called back the dragon.

After that, the twins didn't talk for a while. The rain was getting worse as they climbed. And the trail was becoming narrower, and kind of tricky.

Suddenly, Roy's boot slipped in the mud. Amy reached for him as he got his balance back.

"You okay?" Amy asked worriedly.

Roy looked over his shoulder and nodded, then forced a smile. But his face was a little pale—the misstep at such a steep height had shaken him.

The storm was getting really bad. The wind pulled at their bodies. Amy looked up. The caves were only a dozen feet above them. If they climbed straight up, they could be there in no time.

"I'm gonna try going up," she said.

Before Roy could stop her, Amy started climbing. She grabbed hold of some jagged rocks sticking out of the coarse mountainside and hauled herself up.

"Amy, you're gonna get yourself killed!"

She climbed higher, ignoring her twin brother's warning. "You're just bugged that I took the lead!"

Annoyed, Roy started to climb after her.

Halfway up, a rock shifted under Amy's hand. Fear spiraled inside her. She found a better grip instantly and kept going.

Just don't look down, she told herself. *Whatever you do, don't look down.*

Then she looked down.

A terrifying drop greeted her, straight into the

pearl gray mist that hugged the side of the mountain. They were up so high, hundreds of feet. If the view had been clear, she might have been able to see Crestview, the orphanage that had been her home since she was five. But the blanket of fog was too thick.

Thunder crashed and the mountain shook. Amy gasped as small rocks fell from above. One hit her in the shoulder.

"Are you okay?" Roy called up.

"Yeah," she said. Her voice was small and weak.

"Um...Why don't you tell me about your dream?" Roy asked.

"You—you don't want to hear about my dream. You think dreams are stupid."

"That's never stopped you before."

Amy felt a slight flush in her cheeks. Then she smiled and started climbing again. "It was like I was on some island. And there were dinosaurs everywhere. Want me to show you?"

"Maybe later," Roy said.

"Oh," she said, remembering the way he'd jumped when she put the image of the dragon in his head. "Right. It was like...well, like I wasn't the one having the dream. I was someone else. One of the dinosaurs. And I was playing this game."

"Tell me how warm it was again," Roy said. His teeth were starting to chatter.

Amy gently eased the sensation of warmth from her dream into his thoughts.

"Wow—that *is* nice," he said. "Sorry I had to wake you up."

The thunder came again. Louder. Closer this time. There was the sharp crackle of lightning and bright light cast the world in black and white for an instant.

"That's weird," Roy said. He had almost caught up to her on the climb.

"What?"

"The lightning was farther off. That means the storm should be breaking. And the rain's starting to ease off. But the thunder keeps getting stronger—"

The booming sound came again. It was louder than ever. The mountain vibrated. Dirt and stone came down on them. But neither lost their hand- or footholds. The ledge leading to one of the caves was only a few feet above.

"This doesn't make sense," Roy said.

Amy was no longer paying attention. The ledge was within her reach now. She grabbed hold and started pulling herself up.

Suddenly, the rock she'd been grasping broke away from the ledge. She felt as if she were being yanked out into open air. She heard Roy shout her name. Felt his terror. But he wasn't the one who was falling.

She was.

CHAPTER

2

Amy screamed as she plummeted, turning and twisting in the air, her hands grasping wildly. Then, in a flash, a wall of mist seemed to rise up and snatch her.

An instant later, she hit something hard with a loud grunt of pain.

The mist was still all around her. But at least she could see what she'd landed on, and it certainly wasn't the ground.

The ground wasn't charcoal gray, unless it was the aftermath of a forest fire. And the ground wasn't leathery and moist and weirdly cushionlike. And it didn't have this *smell*, either.

Amy coughed. What was that odor? It was like something she'd smelled in science lab when the teacher brought in a bunch of frogs.

But if she wasn't lying on the ground, then what *was* she lying on?

Amy touched her arms and legs. She was sore and bruised, but otherwise unhurt. She sat up and saw that she was on some kind of ledge. It wasn't wide. Maybe ten feet. And there were sharp things sticking up at the end of it. If she didn't know better, she would have said they were animal claws.

"Roy!" she shouted. "Roy! I'm okay!"

She knew it was useless to yell. So, instead, she reached out with her telepathic power—

Then quickly pulled back. Something was out there. Something *living*…something in the mist.

Amy didn't know what it was, but she *his* thoughts weren't like a human's or *an* animal's—none she had ever known, any*se* thoughts were different. Alien, somehow. *r.*

Suddenly, the ledge moved. Amy was thre *ff* balance. She grabbed onto one of the bone white sharp things for support and felt it budge a little.

"Oh…" she whispered.

The ledge that wasn't a ledge at all started rising up. As it did, another shape came out of the mists, a *head* the size of a two-story building!

Amy looked into the face of Godzilla—and suddenly wasn't the least bit afraid anymore. She could feel what he was feeling. *Curiosity.*

In one of his huge dark eyes she could see her

own reflection: a tiny brown-haired girl with a proud but pleasant face and shining blue eyes. Her clothes were too big for her thin form—the orphanage had to rely on donations—yet somehow she radiated strength and courage. And her soul was filled with the same longings as the creature's.

"It was *your* dream," she whispered to the giant. "The dinosaurs in the hot place. The games."

Amy used her power to gently place images from the dream she'd had into Godzilla's mind.

Godzilla roared with delight. Amy held onto his claw, yelling, "Whoa! Don't shake like that!"

Godzilla got the message. He held her steady.

Amy gazed at Godzilla, wondering how he'd gotten up to the state of Washington. She'd heard news reports weeks before about his appearance in Los Angeles and his flight to the Nevada desert. She remembered something about Godzilla trashing Las Vegas, too, but she never thought he'd come up to her home state.

"What are you doing up here?" Amy asked. She didn't really expect a reply—not in human terms anyway.

Instead, images brushed against her thoughts. She saw Godzilla wading to shore from the Pacific Ocean. Then she saw him fighting men in terrible war machines. Then she saw Godzilla wandering across the countryside, searching for something...

and, finally, she saw Godzilla curled up in the ocean depths, happy and dreaming.

"You're lost," Amy said. "You want to find your way back to your home deep in the sea."

Godzilla looked at her expectantly.

"I'll help. At least, I can try to point you in the direction of the ocean. But...would you do something for me first?"

The one-hundred-meter-tall giant waited as Amy began to recall times she'd spent with Billy, the young runaway. She then placed images of the boy inside Godzilla's mind.

Godzilla nodded slowly, and Amy felt him responding. She let Godzilla's thoughts become her own.

Gradually, she found herself looking at an image of Billy. He was cold, wet, and curled up and shivering in a dark place. He hugged a frayed old Cat in the Hat stuffed toy. A candy bar wrapper peeked out of his torn jeans.

"But where is he exactly?" whispered Amy.

The picture suddenly pulled back, and Amy could now see that Billy was hiding in a cave—a deep purple gash in the side of the mountain.

Amy recognized the place. It was on the other side of the mountain.

The view from Godzilla's eyes melted away. Amy once again found herself looking up at her colossal gray-scaled companion.

"We need to get Roy first," Amy said as she pointed up to the place where she'd fallen.

Godzilla grunted happily, as if this was a game. He carried her gently in the direction she pointed, through the thick mist.

When Amy came in sight of her brother, his eyes went wide.

"Amy!" he cried as he watched her drifting toward him out of the mist.

She could feel her brother's relief.

Roy shook his head. Tears welled in the corners of his eyes. "I thought—I thought—"

"I'm okay," she said. "I hitched a ride."

She watched as he looked down at the moving gray slab she sat upon.

"I don't get it," he said.

Roy's mind raced with all kinds of weird possibilities as he tried to make sense of what he was seeing. What the heck was carrying his sister? A magic carpet made of stone?

No, that's crazy, Roy told himself. Sure, he loved reading about magical adventures in faraway places, but that stuff wasn't *real*.

Maybe she was on some kind of platform attached to a crane? Roy decided. But if it was, then what were those clawlike things that kept wriggling? And, more importantly, what was that gargantuan shape moving behind Amy?

Suddenly, Godzilla's form broke fully through the thick mist. Roy stared at the giant who was carrying his sister. He knew Godzilla was real. He'd seen footage of the monster on the news. But it was one thing to know something in your *mind*—and quite another to come face to face with it in *reality!*

He stood paralyzed, mouth agape.

"Roy! Climb on!" Amy said with a laugh.

He shook his head, his face pale.

"Godzilla won't hurt us. Come on. He's seen Billy."

The giant claw moved close to the ledge.

"Is this for real?" Roy asked. "I mean—I mean—"

"See for yourself."

Hesitantly, Roy touched one of Godzilla's claws. It wriggled slightly. Roy began to fidget. His breath made little white clouds. He rubbed his hands.

Trying not to look down, he stepped into Godzilla's waiting palm. "I can't believe I'm doing this," he muttered.

Amy smiled. She focused her power and sent more images of Billy into Godzilla's mind—along with feelings of being lost, frightened, and alone. Billy's feelings.

Godzilla roared. He took a few thundering steps, and Amy and Roy recognized those same booming sounds they'd heard earlier—the sounds they'd *thought* had been coming from the storm clouds!

Roy grabbed hold of his stomach. "I think I'm getting seasick..."

Amy whooped and hollered. She loved the ride.

As Godzilla circled the mountain, the mists began to part and the rain lightened. Amy looked down and spotted the orphanage in the distance. She pointed it out to Roy.

"I wish we didn't have to take him back there," her brother said.

"Billy was just upset because that family changed their minds about adopting him. He thinks no one's ever going to want him. No one cares."

"He shouldn't think that," Roy said.

Amy shrugged. She lightly tapped his forehead. "There's a big difference between what people know"—she moved her hand over his heart—"and what they feel."

"I guess," Roy admitted. He looked over the side. "Hey, check it out! Godzilla's tail!"

Amy looked over the edge of Godzilla's palm and saw the giant's tail whipping back and forth. It struck a couple of trees, and they exploded into splinters!

"I think Godzilla should hire out for demolition work," Roy said.

Amy laughed and shook her head. "You would."

Then Amy recognized the purple gash in the side

of the mountain. She pointed at the cave entrance, and Godzilla took them right to it. They climbed down from his palm and entered the dark cavern.

Roy took a flashlight out of the bag he carried. As he shone the beam inside the cave, a rustling sounded.

"Billy?" Amy said. "It's me. Amy."

The sound came again.

"Don't be scared," Roy said. "We've got some food. Are you hungry?"

A snuffling sound reached out from the darkness.

"You have a cold?" Amy asked.

Suddenly, a towering figure lunged out of the darkness. Flashing white claws and teeth, dark wet fur, and wild eyes rushed toward them.

A bear! Amy was too surprised to use her powers. Even the level-headed Roy was frozen.

The animal was almost upon the twins when a shadow fell over them. A blinding light flared at Amy and Roy's backs, along with a fiery heat. A thunderous roar made them jump.

The bear scampered back into the darkness. Amy and Roy turned to see Godzilla leaning down. His face was level with the cave's mouth. A bright silver fire glowed in his maw. A warning.

"Oh, no..." Roy whispered. "If Billy was sleeping in that bear's cave—"

"*Billy!*" Amy cried loudly.

"Up here!" came a small voice from above.

Amy and Roy looked up. Billy was peeking out of a cave ten feet above them. His face was filthy, his clothes a mess.

"Will you take me home?" he asked.

Godzilla reached out a claw. Billy stared at him and blinked in fright.

"Don't be scared, Billy. He's our new friend," called Amy. "Just climb on!"

Billy swallowed uncertainly before finally climbing on. Godzilla lowered his claw to Amy and Roy next. Amy leaped on and gave Billy a big hug.

Then she looked the six-year-old in the eye and said, "Billy, you've got to promise me something. No matter how bad things get, you can't—"

"Running away stinks," Billy said. "It was cold, and I didn't have anything to eat, and there wasn't anyone I could talk to—"

"I think he's got it down," Roy said as he stepped onto Godzilla's palm and looked up at the giant's face. "Why do you think Godzilla's helping us?"

"Because we're friends," Amy said, patting one of his fingers. "Right, big guy?"

She sent a flood of warm thoughts into Godzilla's mind. He made a low *thrummmmming* sound. His claw shook just a little with the vibrations.

"Okay," Amy said. "Going down!"

Godzilla's hand swept through the air. Amy

noticed Roy getting a little green.

"You gotta admit, this is the only way to travel," Amy teased.

"Oh, yeah," he said, holding his stomach as they swayed through the air and rapidly descended. It might as well have been an amusement park ride!

Then he noticed Billy. The boy had curled up with a relieved smile on his face. The swaying motion had lulled him instantly to sleep.

Godzilla crouched down and lowered his claw as close as he could to the ground. Roy picked up Billy. He carefully stepped off Godzilla's palm and onto a winding, tree-lined trail.

Roy's legs were a little wobbly. He was grateful to be on solid ground once more.

"Are we there yet?" Billy murmured.

"Almost," Roy answered, even though he knew it would be another hour's walk to the orphanage.

Amy looked around. The mist was heavier down here at the mountain's base. And now she could hear odd sounds. There were other shapes moving in the mist. Cars or trucks.

"Rescue vans!" Roy said. "They must have decided to check the mountain after all."

Amy felt something was wrong. "I don't think so."

Godzilla let out a low growl. His towering body tensed. Seconds later, he was under attack!

CHAPTER

3

Amy could hardly believe what she was seeing. Fighter jets swooped in and fired on Godzilla. Tanks rolled near the towering creature and shot cannon shells at him. They exploded against his skin and bathed him in glowing green fire.

Godzilla roared and stumbled back. He fell against the mountain, and the earth trembled with the impact. The fiery emerald energy threatened to engulf him!

The psychic bond Amy had established with Godzilla let her feel his pain and confusion. He had been struck by greater weapons than these and shrugged off any ill effects. Why were these weapons hurting him so badly?

It came to both Amy and Godzilla at the exact same instant: *The green fire.*

"Roy!" she called to her brother. "We've got to do something!"

Roy was still carrying Billy. Miraculously, all the noise hadn't woken up the six-year-old. He was tired enough to sleep through anything, even a battle that sounded like World War Three.

"Roy, please!" Amy cried.

Frowning, Roy ignored his sister's desperate plea. They had to get clear of the danger. He hurried past Amy, then stopped as he realized she wasn't following.

"We have to go!" Roy called back to his twin sister. "This isn't safe!"

"We have to help Godzilla!"

"Amy, get real. *We're just kids.* What can we do?"

"I don't know yet, but we've got to try!"

Roy was going to argue further, but he knew how stubborn his sister could be. Then he looked down at the boy in his arms and thought of one way to get Amy moving. "What about Billy? We've got to think about his safety."

Amy frowned, then hung her head. "You're right," she said in defeat.

The sound of falling rocks made the twins look up. Amy's eyes widened as she saw Godzilla dig

22

one of his claws into the mountainside and shower rocks down on two of the tanks fifty yards away.

Then the monster opened his maw and bathed one of the fighter jets with bright blue-white atomic flame. The craft veered off and crashed against the mountain. The pilot's ejection parachute opened in the sky seconds before the impact.

More tanks and jets arrived. Missiles exploded against Godzilla. Fire raced over him, and Amy felt him getting weaker with every hit.

"Amy, *now* would be good!" Roy shouted. Smoke had replaced the mist at the base of the mountain. It was getting harder to see the path before them. "We've gotta *go!*"

But before either of them could take a step, a Japanese man came out of the smoke surrounding them. He was tall and handsome, and he wore a leather jacket, blue jeans, and black leather boots. Peeking out from underneath his unzipped jacket was a Mighty Mouse T-shirt.

"Yes, the boy is right," the man said. "I don't know what you two are doing here, but those shells are attuned to Godzilla's DNA. They'll take him down—and if we're not careful, he'll take us with him."

"Who are you?" asked Amy.

"I'm Dr. Hiro Kuroyama," said the man. "I'm a kaijuologist."

"A *kye-ju-olo*—what?" asked Roy.

"*Kaiju* means 'monster' in Japanese. We don't have time for lengthy explanations. Let's just say I study everything about giant creatures, their biology, behavior, origins—"

Amy's psychic ability was stronger than Roy's. She used it to burrow into the young scientist's mind. Instantly, she discovered what had caused this attack on Godzilla.

"You're wrong about Godzilla!" Amy cried. "And so is the military! You've all made a mistake! Godzilla wasn't trying to hurt us. He saved my life and he helped us find Billy!"

The man looked at her strangely. "You can read my thoughts?"

She nodded sharply. "Both of us can."

"Then you know there's nothing I can do to call off the attack. We've been following Godzilla through these mountains for days. General Cutwell's been looking for an excuse to go after him with everything he's got. Seeing him reaching for you kids gave him just what he was looking for. Now come on, before it's too late."

"You heard him," Roy said. "Move!"

Amy couldn't take a step. She was stunned. It was *her* fault. If she had just let Godzilla go his way, none of this would have happened.

All of a sudden, a strange feeling came to her. It

felt as if other entities were coming closer. At once, Amy realized that Godzilla wasn't alone.

A moment later, the ground shook as a figure rounded the left flank of the mountain and leaped onto one of the tanks. It was a giant lizard!

"Varan," Hiro whispered in disbelief. "I thought we'd left him behind in the desert with the others."

"What others?" asked Roy.

"Desert creatures mutated by a research accident," explained the scientist. "It all happened weeks ago at a secret facility in Nevada—"

Suddenly, more monsters appeared. A giant praying mantis flew through the sky and tore the wing off one of the planes. A spider several stories high leaped down from the mountain toward the soldiers. Hiro called the giant praying mantis "Kamacuras" and the huge spider "Kumonga."

Next, the ground trembled as a twenty-foot-tall gopher stuck out its six-foot head. It bounded from the tunnel it had dug, and a collection of smaller creatures chased after it. Hiro recognized a five-foot-long armadillo and three fifteen-foot-long lizards—one looked like a gecko, the second a Gila monster, and the third a chuckwalla.

Finally, a terrible rattling filled the air as a super-giant rattlesnake slithered down one side of the mountain, while another serpent, a huge coral snake with bright yellow markings on its black and

red body, appeared behind the military. "Rattler" and "Yellowback" were as long as freight trains, and they wrapped their powerful, monstrous bodies around the remaining tanks, holding them firm.

Dozens of escape hatches popped open on the tanks, and terrified soldiers leaped from them to safety. Then Kumonga, the spider, moved in and pierced each of the tanks with his daggerlike legs, effortlessly ripping the machines to pieces.

Amy looked up and saw Godzilla back on his feet. The monster army had saved Godzilla's life. Now the spines on his back were glowing with a silver-white light, and she knew he was going to let loose his atomic flame!

With an angry roar, Godzilla advanced on the now helpless soldiers.

"No!" Amy cried. She had to find a way to calm Godzilla, to stop him.

Amy gritted her teeth and closed her eyes. Concentrating harder than she ever had in her life, she re-created the dinosaur world from Godzilla's dream and sent it into his mind.

For Godzilla, the soldiers and their weapons faded away and were replaced by images from the dream. And they were more than images. Godzilla could *feel* the heat of the sun, *smell* the damp air, *hear* his friends call to him. And he was at peace.

"I can see it, too," Roy said. "Dinosaurs!"

"So can I," Hiro said. "Is that an island?"

Amy was pleased that Godzilla was calm. But she knew it was temporary. Behind it, a flaming wall of anger was waiting to erupt again.

"Why?" Amy asked the monster. She sensed Godzilla's anger came from a place much deeper than the events of today. "Why are you so angry?"

Suddenly, Amy was overwhelmed by an explosion of images and feelings that left her breathless. She saw Godzilla as he had been once. A Godzillasaurus, the last of his kind. Then the blinding flash of light had come, the explosion from the atomic bomb.

Agony overwhelmed him as the bomb's fallout changed him, mutating him from a dinosaur into a dinosaur *monster*—a freak, destined to live alone, feared by everything in nature.

Humans had been responsible for his monstrous transformation. Somehow, Godzilla had always sensed this. And now they were attacking him again!

Amy opened her eyes and saw Godzilla staring down at her. His fury was beginning to return.

"Doctor," Amy said quickly, "you have to get those people out of there. Make the soldiers go away. Hurry!"

Hiro didn't stop to question. He pulled a radio out of his jacket and pressed a red button on the side. "General, this is Hiro. We need a full evac. Right now!"

The general wasn't pleased, but something about Hiro's tone made him agree. In moments, the force was retreating. The planes left the area.

Hiro put his hand on Amy's shoulder. She looked up into his face and blinked. Until now, she hadn't noticed just how cute the young scientist was.

"Amy, help me," said Hiro. "Ask Godzilla what else he wants."

Amy watched as all the other giant monsters gathered around Godzilla: Kumonga, the spider; Kamacuras, the praying mantis; Gopher; the two snakes, Rattler and Yellowback; and the others.

Godzilla looked at them all with curiosity. One of the larger monsters came closer to Godzilla. He was the lizardlike creature that Hiro called Varan.

Varan was about thirty meters tall. Pretty big, but still less than one-third Godzilla's one-hundred-meter height! All at once, he charged Godzilla, giving him a friendly head butt. Godzilla rocked on his feet, his tail keeping him from falling down. Then Godzilla returned the gesture, and Varan landed on his backside, making the ground tremble.

The other monsters began to hop and slither with a kind of happy excitement. The smaller creatures played near Godzilla's tail, leaping over or beneath it.

"You don't have to be psychic to figure out what Godzilla wants," Roy said. "Look at him with those other monsters. He's not alone anymore. He's happy."

"All he needs now is a place to call home," Amy said. "Come to think of it," she added with a glance to her twin brother, "that's all any of us needs."

Hiro thought about this idea of Godzilla wanting a home. "I do know of an uncharted island in the South Pacific," he said.

"An island?" said Roy.

"Yes. Two giant creatures are already living on the island, being observed by a scientific team. It's a kind of *kaiju* habitat. I studied there once."

"Yeah," said Roy, "but how do you get Godzilla there?"

Hiro nodded. "Yes, that's a problem. We could never cage him. He's too big. The only thing we could possibly do is lead him there. But how do we get him to follow?"

Amy grinned. "I can think of a way."

"Amy—" Roy warned, guessing what she was going to say.

But Amy ignored her brother. Staring into Hiro's eyes, she said, "All you have to do is take us along with you!"

CHAPTER

4

Godzilla had no idea what to do.

He'd been in the presence of other monsters before. But it had never been like *this*. There were so many! And they all seemed to want some-thing from him.

What?

Did they think he could lead them to food? Shelter? He had no idea where to find such things. He just wandered until he came across them.

Cries of joy came from his feet. Godzilla looked down at the smaller monsters. They only wanted to play. Godzilla watched them chase each other. He could tell they were very young.

A roar sounded. Godzilla lifted his gaze. The older monsters looked him in the eye. Godzilla sensed they'd been trying to find him for some time. And now that they had, they expected him to give them what they had come for.

Godzilla decided he'd try to communicate in the Old Way. He chose the giant lizard Varan. Godzilla nudged Varan's shoulder and lightly closed his jaws over the side of his neck. Then he withdrew.

Nothing. Varan had stood his ground, hadn't seemed afraid...but he also didn't appear to understand how to respond to this simple question, either.

Godzilla decided to try something else. He vibrated his tail at just the right speed and whipped it back and forth a few times. The little monsters scattered. The rattlesnake looked upset. A sharp rattling filled the air.

Varan simply didn't get it.

Godzilla roared with frustration. He looked around for something to smash. Kamacuras and Kumonga bounced up and down in excitement.

Suddenly, Godzilla felt a warm, delicious tingling in his mind. The bright-faced girl was back! Her thoughts were pure. Like music.

Images filled his mind. He saw a beautiful island. The plants were like those he had sometimes nibbled on when he'd been small. A creature wandered nearby.

Godzilla recognized it—an armored dinosaur with many spikes. Only this one was huge.

Changed somehow. Just as he had been.

Within his mind, a cry sounded from above. Godzilla looked up and was stunned to see a pterosaur—a golden-bellied flier with an enormous wingspan.

If only this were real. Something more than a dream...

Godzilla looked down and saw the girl walking next to the Ankylosaurus. She was nodding. Smiling. Gesturing for him to come with her.

If a place like this really existed, he would go through anything to reach it.

The dream faded, and Godzilla looked around. The other monsters had shared his vision. They began to hop with excitement. Godzilla now understood what they wanted. It was the same thing that he wanted.

A home.

And they wanted *him* to lead them to it.

"Amy, can you hear me?" Roy asked.

Amy shook herself. Her vision cleared. She smiled at Roy. "It's just kinda freaky. Going into their heads."

She looked down at the photographs of Rodan and Anguirus that Hiro had given her. He said he'd taken the pictures when he was studying on their island.

"Godzilla understands about going to the island," she told Hiro and the gray-haired general who'd joined him. "He thinks Rodan and Anguirus are dinosaurs who were changed. Like him."

"He's probably correct," Hiro said.

A Jeep rumbled over to them. Billy was on the passenger side, wrapped up in a blanket. The young soldier driving the Jeep said to Amy and Roy, "The boy wanted to see you two before I took him back to the orphanage."

Amy went to Billy. "Don't worry. It'll be all right."

"You're not coming with me?" Billy cried.

Amy looked to Roy. He looked away uncomfortably. "Not right away," said Amy. "We're going to help Godzilla. But we'll see you again. Don't worry."

"You promise?"

She smiled warmly and nodded. "I promise."

Billy looked at the collection of monsters lining the mountain. "Guess they weren't dragons after all, huh, Amy?"

"You weren't that far off," Amy said. "Are you gonna be all right? You're not gonna run away again, are you?"

Billy shook his head. "I just...are you sure I can't come with you?"

"What? Are you kidding? And miss all the welcome-home parties and stuff they'll be doing for you at Crestview?"

"Parties?"

Amy ruffled the six-year-old's hair. "You bet. Everyone was worried about you."

"Everyone?"

"Sure. And imagine what it's gonna be like for you when you tell all your stories about Godzilla."

Billy smiled as he pictured it. "Yeah, you're right. It'll be *cool.*"

Amy kissed Billy's forehead and motioned for the driver to head on. Behind her, the silver-haired General Cutwell nodded. He was smiling, too.

Two of the general's officers arrived. They opened a map and spread it on the ground. The first was a pudgy man with red hair. With him was a younger woman wearing sunglasses. Her long blond hair had been pulled back into a ponytail that flowed from the rear of her camouflage cap.

"This is the route we've picked out," the pudgy man said. His name tag read EDWARDS.

The female officer traced the route with a finger. "I think we should follow this tributary to Puget Sound, then go north and then west until we reach the Pacific. If we go this way, we'll avoid civilization and reach the ocean quicker. But it means breaking out the winter jackets. It'll be cold."

The general nodded. "We go north. Fair enough."

The caravan set out almost at once. It was made up

of a half-dozen Jeeps, two tanks, and a single helicopter.

Godzilla and his new giant friends didn't like the
helicopter—they kept taking swipes at it—so the
pilot kept a fair distance away. A squadron of fight-
ers was kept on alert at a nearby air force base.

Amy, Roy, and Hiro sat in the back of an open
Jeep so Godzilla could see them and follow along.

They didn't have to do much to lead the other
monsters. Wherever Godzilla went, they went,
too.

"I feel sorry for anybody trying to drive on these
roads after we're through with them," Roy cracked.
"Godzilla's leaving potholes the size of a bus!"

Hiro glanced at Amy. "Is your brother always like
this?"

She smiled. "Usually, he's worse."

The day wore on, and Amy, Roy, and Hiro found
ways to make the time pass. Amy pulled out a
deck of cards and, in the middle of the afternoon,
she challenged the young scientist to a game of
Hearts.

"I don't know if I should be doing this," the scientist said. "Playing cards with someone who can
read my mind."

Amy giggled. She was really beginning to like
Hiro. He was so handsome. And clever. And funny.

Get a grip, will you? Roy whispered inside her

head. *Like Hiro's gonna go for a shrimp like you. He's old enough to—*

Amy whipped around and punched her brother in the shoulder. Hard.

"Ow!" he cried. "What'd you do that for?"

"You know exactly why!" Amy said. "Jerk."

Hiro watched them. He guessed that Roy had been using his powers in a way Amy didn't like.

Suddenly, a bellow came from the collection of monsters behind them. Varan had kicked one of the smaller monsters racing around his feet.

Godzilla growled a warning, and Varan lowered his head.

Hiro took note of this and wondered if there was a connection between what Amy and Roy felt and the way the monsters were acting.

By sunset, the caravan had reached the tributary river. Amy had to do a little coaxing, but Godzilla and his friends gradually moved into the water.

High waves sloshed over the riverbanks as water was displaced by the huge monsters. The vehicles had to keep moving back from the river's edge to avoid being swept away.

"Well, at least getting them off land should help cut down on the property damage," Roy remarked. "They were really tearing up the roads."

"That's only part of the reason," Hiro explained.

"It's easier to keep the waterways clear than the highways. And it makes sense to keep as far away as we can from populated areas."

"That's a *good* idea, Hiro," Amy said.

Hiro noticed the way Amy's eyelids fluttered as she looked at him. He rubbed his chin uneasily, wondering what it meant.

Amy looked up and saw yet another news helicopter buzz toward the monsters. The military chopper chased it off.

Amy, I hope you're kidding, Roy said through her mind. *Or should I just tell Hiro you've got a crush on him—*

"Shut up!" Amy yelled. She launched herself at her brother and they started wrestling. He caught her wrists to keep her from hitting him again.

"Kids!" Hiro said. "Kids, stop it!"

"See?" Roy taunted. "You're just a kid!"

"I'm gonna bust you up!" Amy cried, freeing one hand and starting to whale on him.

Hiro hauled her away from her brother. They fell back, and the scientist had to put his arms around Amy to keep her from falling off the Jeep.

"Oh," Amy said, suddenly calming down. Hiro watched her eyes widen and her eyelids flutter at him again. He sighed, hoping this wasn't what it looked like—a schoolgirl crush.

Suddenly, a roar came from the water. Kamacuras and Kumonga were fighting. And the monster snakes were, too. Rattler and Yellowback were both dipping in and out of the water, emerging only long enough to snap at each other's heads.

Hiro gently deposited Amy on her seat.

"Amy, Roy, look at what you're doing!" Hiro exclaimed. He pointed at the monsters.

"What are you talking about? *We* didn't do anything," Roy argued.

"No, Roy. Hiro's right." Amy reached out with her power. "The monsters are acting on *our* feelings."

"Please, Amy," Hiro said. "If there's any way you can help to calm them down—"

Hiro's radio crackled. He picked it up. "Hiro here."

"Dead ahead, Doctor!" came the soldier's voice.

Hiro stared into the darkness. For an instant, he saw nothing. Then he realized what the soldier on the other side of the radio was talking about.

There was a bridge dead ahead, stretched over the river! All of its lights had been turned off. But the helicopter swooped down low, using its spotlight to reveal the bridge and the hundreds of sightseers who had gathered there to see the monsters.

The onlookers were about to get a really good view, because the monsters were heading right for the bridge—on a direct collision course!

CHAPTER

5

Hiro looked at the maps ne'd been shown. The bridge hadn't been on any of them. As the entire caravan slowed to a stop, Hiro picked up his radio and changed the frequency.

"General," Hiro said urgently. "We've got a situation."

As Hiro listened to General Cutwell's response, he saw Amy looking to her brother. Roy appeared genuinely sorry for the way he'd acted before.

"I don't know if I can do this by myself," Amy said softly.

"I'll help. Just tell me what to do," Roy said.

Hiro wasn't sure he liked the sound of that. "General, I'll get back with you."

Ignoring General Cutwell's blustering, Hiro

switched off the radio and dropped it into his pocket. He looked to Amy and Roy. Their faces were tight masks of concentration.

Amy's eyes were going slightly out of focus, as they always did before she used her power. "Just keep an eye on me."

Roy nodded. "Yeah."

"Wait," Hiro said. "We can't be impulsive now. Listen—"

But it was too late. Amy had closed her eyes. Hiro could feel a kind of crackling static energy in his mind. She was using her power, directing it at Godzilla.

"Amy, can you hear me?" Hiro asked.

In a kind of trance, Amy said, "I can hear you."

"We have to be careful. Very careful—"

Amy didn't seem to be listening to Hiro. Instead she said, "Godzilla's angry. He doesn't know why, but he's angry. Maybe it's because of the way the new monsters are acting. Fighting and snapping and attacking each other for no good reason."

Hiro thought about this. Amy's mood *had* affected the temperaments of Godzilla and the others. They'd picked up on her emotions. Hiro wondered if he could use that fact to their advantage. He had to try.

"Amy, this is what I want you to do," Hiro said. "I want you to think about the most calm, relaxing times you've ever had. Can you do that?"

"Lying in a field," she murmured. "Looking at the clouds. Feeling the summer breezes."

"Good." Hiro could hear the roars of Godzilla and the others. They were closing in on the bridge. Soldiers were shouting. Hiro heard something about an air strike, and he knew there wasn't much time now.

"Amy, concentrate on that feeling of calm," Hiro said. "This is very important, and—"

"I'm *trying*," she snapped.

Hiro frowned. That was a mistake. He shouldn't have let Amy hear his worry. Now she'd think he didn't believe in her, and that would make her tense.

Hiro looked to the monsters. They were still making threatening noises at one another. Amy needed help. Hiro looked to her brother. "Roy, can you—"

Roy nodded before Hiro even finished. "Come on, Amy, get calm. Think about that week we spent down on the islands with Mom and Dad. We were jammin', mon!"

Amy laughed. "Yeah, those were good times."

Hiro was amazed, yet again, that Amy's powers could even make him begin to feel the heat of the sun, the softness of the white sand, the gentle lullaby of the waves from just beyond the shore.

Hiro looked up and saw that Godzilla had calmed down. But he was the only one.

"The other monsters are still moving," Hiro said, unable to control his concern. "Still heading for the bridge!"

"I'm *trying!*" Amy cried again. She trembled with frustration.

Hiro placed a hand on her shoulder. "I'm sorry. Tell me what Godzilla is feeling."

Amy took a deep breath. "He likes wading through the water. He sees the bridge, but figures it'll be just fine to go through it. He could use some exercise."

"You've got to make him understand what'll happen to those people," Hiro insisted. "Amy—"

She responded instantly. Suddenly, Hiro felt the crackling in his mind. He was overwhelmed by Amy's images of people yelling and screaming, falling into the water, panic and fear.

Hiro shuddered. The images stopped. He looked to Godzilla. The towering beast looked startled.

"He hadn't realized," Amy said. "Hadn't thought of the people."

Godzilla looked around at the other monsters and gestured to the shore. They would go around the bridge.

Hiro sat back in the Jeep. The crackling he'd felt in his mind vanished. "Good job, Amy."

Amy sagged in her seat. Roy rubbed Amy's shoulders. She patted his hand.

Suddenly, a loud honking pierced the night. Hiro spun to look at the bridge. The people were honking their horns. Dozens of them! Cheering and flashing portable spotlights at the monsters. Trying to get their attention. And succeeding.

"What are they doing?" Hiro asked. "They're crazy! They'll get themselves *killed!*"

All the monsters turned at the sound. It was as if a new game had begun. Godzilla ignored the sounds and the lights. He turned and started toward the shore. Varan followed him.

Then a sharp, angry rattling filled the air. Godzilla looked back and saw the rattlesnake rear up out of the water and hiss defiantly. Rattler undulated toward the bridge. Yellowback, who had been fighting him only a few moments earlier, went to the rattlesnake's side. With a grunt, Varan followed.

"Whoa!" Roy said, rearing back in his seat. He clutched his skull. "Even *I* felt that one."

"What is it?" Hiro asked. He didn't turn to look at the twelve-year-old. The scientist couldn't take his eyes off the scene unfolding before him.

"Yellowback and Rattler. They're giving in to their instincts. They sense prey on the bridge. So they want to wrap themselves around it and squeeze."

"I understand," Hiro said. He didn't want to contemplate what would come afterward. "But what about Varan? Why is he following?"

"Well…" Roy began. "Don't get me wrong. I like Varan and all. But he's kind of a monster of very little brain."

"Oh," Hiro said. He frowned. "We've got to do something. Amy?"

There was no reply. Hiro turned, wondering why she didn't answer. He saw an empty space beside Roy.

Amy was gone.

Godzilla was very angry. Rattler, Yellowback, and the big lizard Varan didn't care if they hurt people. Only the praying mantis, Kamacuras, and the spider, Kumonga, remained at his side.

With an angry roar and a burst of his atomic fire, Godzilla let the other monsters know he wasn't happy!

The rattler ignored him. But the humans on the bridge made more of their annoying noises. And they flashed more of their unsettling lights.

The bridge only came up to Godzilla's knee. He was a few paces away from it now and knew he had to be careful with his tail. One good swipe was all it would take to smash it.

He got in front of the bridge before the snakes and their big friend could reach it. Kumonga and Kamacuras stood on either side of him.

Godzilla looked around for the little creatures.

The gila, the armadillo, the one that made the funny clicking sound, and the other two were huddled near the opposite shore. Afraid.

That *really* made Godzilla mad. The snakes were scaring the littlest monsters!

Suddenly, Yellowback reared up out of the water, right in front of Godzilla. He hissed a warning. Godzilla leaned forward and opened his mouth. Atomic energy came out in a sizzling display of crackling blue and silver flame!

Yellowback dove under the water. Godzilla's fiery breath baked the surface of the water, turning much of it to rising steam. A mist rose up, making it hard to see, but Godzilla knew Yellowback was fast enough to escape. He just wanted his slithering opponent to know he was serious.

Suddenly, Godzilla felt something brush against his leg. The *other* snake, Rattler, was trying to glide past him to reach the bridge. Godzilla raised his foot and stomped down! Godzilla felt the body of Rattler beneath his foot. He'd trapped him!

Godzilla was careful not to squash Rattler, but he made sure he wasn't going anywhere. There was a terrible thrashing, and Rattler's head burst from the water! He hissed and rattled, but there was nothing else he could do.

Next a shape came straight for Godzilla. He'd forgotten about Varan!

Kamacuras suddenly leaped into Varan's path. With a head butt that sounded like a thunderclap, the giant pryaing mantis crashed into Varan's chest.

The battling giants both fell on the shore, where the little moving boxes filled with humans were lined up. The two-leggers scattered as their boxes flew into the air. One exploded! A yellow fireball rose into the sky!

The bright-faced girl! thought Godzilla suddenly.

He knew that she'd been riding in one of those boxes. Godzilla's head lurched frantically right then left. He had to know where she was, that she was all right! But no matter where he looked, he couldn't see her.

Suddenly, a shape rose up. Yellowback again! Kumonga tried to intercept him, but Yellowback was too crafty. He slithered in the direction of the spidery Kumonga, then moved sharply past him. Fake-out!

Quickly, Yellowback wrapped himself around Godzilla and started to *squeeze.*

Godzilla struggled with Yellowback, but he wouldn't let go. His mouth opened to reveal long fangs, dripping with venom. And then he bit Godzilla!

As Godzilla began to feel faint, one thought consumed him: Where was the bright-faced girl?

CHAPTER

6

Amy was on the bridge. She knew that she'd acted impulsively again, but *someone* had to tell these people to leave while they could!

"You've got to evacuate the bridge!" Amy screamed. "You've got to get off *now!*"

There were families here. Couples. Kids. Everyone either ignored her or didn't hear her. She thought of using her power, but she felt too drained to try.

Around her, the sound of car horns was deafening. She looked at all the pickup trucks and noticed the license plates. These people weren't from around here, she realized. She looked at more plates and could hardly believe it. These people had *all* come from the same place!

Amy looked at the way they dressed. They wore

Godzilla T-shirts. Godzilla hats. Godzilla buttons. They carried big signs with I LOVE GODZILLA! written in big green glow-in-the-dark letters.

Maybe Hiro was right, thought Amy. Maybe they *were* crazy.

She walked up to a couple. The man was a little overweight. He wore a baseball cap, overalls, and big yellow rubber boots. He sat on the top of his pickup with a bullhorn.

"Yee-haw!" he yelled as the monsters fought in the water just ahead. "You go get 'em, Kumonga!"

The mist was making it tough to see what was going on, but these people didn't seem to mind. Several had video cameras.

"Hey!" Amy cried.

The guy with the bullhorn looked down.

"They're gonna smash the bridge!" Amy said. "Use the bullhorn. Tell everyone!"

The big guy leaned back like he had all the time in the world. "Little darlin'," he began, "it's clear you ain't from our town. Lemme explain. We came a long way just to see old Godzilla. We're not gonna run now. We was hopin' for somethin' like this!"

"Big monster action!" the wife said. She was thin and covered with freckles. "It sells!"

Amy was speechless.

"See, we're hopin' to talk the big guy himself into stompin' our old town, so we can rename it

Godzillaville!" the man in the overalls said. "It'll be a big tourist draw. Lotsa rides! Plenty o' souvenirs!"

His wife touched his shoulder. "Hon, we should think about the feelings of the other monsters. Maybe *Monstertown* would be a better name."

"Well—somethin' like that! Heaven knows, the economy's been bad, and we could use a shot in the arm right about now. No offense, sweetie, but ain't no little girl's gonna change our minds."

They both looked away from her.

That does it. Amy thought she'd been too drained to use her power, but not now!

Amy lashed out with her mind. She blanketed all the people on the bridge with images of the monsters attacking. Hurling pickups *and* people. *Chowing down...*

The effect was immediate.

Screams came from the bridge. The car horns became more frantic. There was no rhythm to them anymore. Only chaos.

For a moment, Amy was pleased with herself. Then she heard the sound of cars and trucks smashing into one another, and she knew she'd made a rash and reckless mistake.

"Look out!" Amy cried.

One of the cars mashed through the protective barrier and came to a sudden, jerky stop. Its front wheels spun over a sheer drop.

Nearby, Varan was on the move. He slammed into the rapidly weakening Godzilla. Godzilla's tail whipped out and hit the bridge, making the roadway sway back and forth like a giant swing.

Amy was tossed off her feet. She saw the car that now sat halfway off the bridge. The driver was yanked out just as the car fell into the water. It hit with a terrible splash.

Amy saw Yellowback untangle himself from Godzilla. The giant snake rose on one side of the bridge, while Rattler escaped from beneath Godzilla's foot and came up on the other side.

A pickup smashed down a few feet near Amy. She turned and saw the couple she'd talked with before. They were inside the pickup, trying to climb out through the passenger-side door, which was now aimed straight up at the stars.

Amy saw the man's bullhorn sitting nearby. She snatched it up and pressed the button on the side. "Leave your cars and trucks and *run!*"

Yellowback's head came right over the top of the couple's truck just as they fled. The snake's jaws bit down on the pickup and lifted it high. He shook it a few times and tossed it into the water.

Amy suddenly smelled something *terrible*. She looked over her shoulder and saw the second snake's head sink down toward her. It was the giant rattler—and she was smelling his breath!

When the snake's deadly rattle sounded, Amy froze. The rattler moved past her and snatched up another truck!

Behind the rattler, Yellowback was winding his body around the bridge. Amy knew the bridge couldn't take the stress. And there were still so many people trapped—

Suddenly, a hissing sound came from the mist. White streaks burst out of the night. They hit Yellowback and stuck to his body. Milky white strands. Dripping with something odd.

The spider! realized Amy. It was his webbing.

Yellowback's body was now being dragged off the bridge by the webbing. He writhed and slapped, but couldn't fight it. A few supports broke loose, and the bridge sagged in the middle.

Then Amy heard a familiar roar.

Godzilla!

He burst through the mist and grabbed the rattler. He shook the troublemaker, then tossed him over the bridge. Kamacuras, the praying mantis, went flying overhead, carrying the spider, Kumonga, who had a firm grasp on the wriggling Yellowback. They vanished into the mist ahead. And from somewhere distant came a pair of loud splashes.

The only one left was Varan. Godzilla faced the lizard. Varan put his head down. Godzilla rammed it. Once. Twice. A third time for good measure.

Then he turned his back and walked up the shore *around* the bridge.

Varan just sort of followed.

Godzilla looked over his shoulder directly at Amy. He raised a single claw triumphantly.

Amy heard voices. She looked around and saw Hiro and Roy. They got her away from the bridge as soldiers moved in to drag the rest of the frightened people to safety.

A few minutes later, the bridge collapsed. It sank into the water. A crowd of people waited on the shore. Many took off their baseball caps and held their heads down.

"Our pickups," one said.

Another turned and hollered, "Thank *goodness* for insurance!"

The whole crowd cheered.

Amy shook her head and turned away.

Hiro put his hand on her shoulder. "The chopper pilot spotted Godzilla and the others heading downstream. We've got a pair of tanks and three Jeeps working. We'd best join the monsters."

Amy felt relieved. Then it occurred to her. "Wait. What about the little guys? The smallest monsters?"

Hiro's expression went blank. "I..."

Amy reached out with her power. Nothing.

"They're gone!" she cried.

CHAPTER

7

That night Hiro and General Cutwell decided that Roy would leave the group with the general and several of his officers. They would search for the smaller monsters who'd run off. Amy would stay with Godzilla and the others to keep them on track.

Amy felt bad about the little guys running off. On the other hand, she looked forward to spending time alone with Hiro.

Only...Hiro was always busy with one thing or another. She didn't even see him again until lunch the next day. The caravan stopped and Hiro hopped up into her Jeep.

For a long time, Hiro didn't say much of anything. Amy tried getting him to talk about books and movies. Even about monsters. Instead, he just ate his portion of the lunch he'd brought to share with her.

Finally, Hiro said, "Amy, I've given this a lot of thought. We need to speak plainly."

"We can talk about anything you want to talk about!" Amy said agreeably.

"You know that your involvement is very important," Hiro said. "We can't communicate with Godzilla unless you're around. He trusts you."

"Thanks," she said, fidgeting happily in her seat.

"Amy, you can't just run off the way you did last night. Your impulsive behavior endangered all of us."

Her smile dropped. "But I *had* to try to help those people on the bridge!"

"Amy, when you and Roy started fighting yesterday, the monsters also started fighting. They respond to your moods. From now on, you must be very careful in what you think and feel."

"Okay, but, I mean…we're still friends, right? You're not mad at me or anything. Right?"

Hiro didn't answer.

"Right?" Amy asked in a small voice.

"I just need you to behave responsibly. Do that, and there will be no problems between us."

"Oh," Amy said. She nodded and looked away. Roy had been right all along, she thought. This wasn't about her actions last night. Hiro was using that as an excuse. He just didn't want to be around her. He didn't like her, that was all.

"The runaway monsters have been spotted at a mall in Seattle. Roy and the general are on their way there. Once they've collected the group of smaller monsters—"

"Whatever," Amy said sharply. She didn't look at Hiro. Didn't want to hear anything he had to say.

"Perhaps you need some time," Hiro said. He took out his radio and commanded the caravan to stop long enough for him to switch to another Jeep.

The pretty young blond officer, Jean Farady, came to keep Amy company. Jean took one look at Amy's hurt expression and said, "Hey, boss. Wanna talk about it?"

"No," Amy said. She fished around among all the toys she'd been given by the military to make the hours pass more quickly. Books on tape. CDs.

None of it interested her. For some reason, all she could think about was Roy. She almost wished her annoying brother was still with them.

By the time Roy and the general got to the three-story mall, things were already out of hand. The local police and National Guard had surrounded the place. Hundreds of people were crushing their way to the exits, and more were inside, trapped by the little posse of monsters.

The leader of the local SWAT team approached the general. "Best way in is through the skylight," the SWAT leader said. His name was Jenkins, and he had brown hair and strong, hard features.

"Get us up there," the general said.

Roy, the general, and the SWAT leader were carried to the roof in a machine called a cherry picker. Jenkins turned to the newcomers. "If you don't mind me asking, General—what's the plan?"

The cherry picker set them down on the roof and they got out. The general looked the SWAT leader in the eye. "Well, Jenkins...the plan is for Roy here to calm these beasties down before they can make lunch out of the people trapped in there."

A half-dozen members of the SWAT team were already on the roof. They had high-tech harnesses with ropes and winches set up.

Roy was nervous, but he tried not to let it show as he was strapped into his harness. He had never had so many people depending on him before. As he looked over the edge of the open skylight, he saw the forty-foot drop waiting for him. "Ugh."

"What is it, son?" the general asked.

"Nothing," Roy said. "It's just...I don't like heights."

The general turned to him and raised a single eyebrow. He was already in his harness. "You know, when I was your age, my favorite book was *Treasure Island.* You know that story?"

Before Roy could reply, the two SWAT guys working on his harness finished up. They checked him over, patted his back, and pulled at the cord attached to him. Each gave a thumbs-up.

"*Treasure Island?*" Roy asked. "Um—yeah. Sure, I've read it. It's great."

"What's your favorite part?"

Roy shrugged. "Off the top of my head? I dunno."

"Well, now, you think about that," the general said. Smiling, he gave Roy a gentle kick in the backside that sent him over the edge.

Roy yelled, but he only went a couple of feet. The harness and its line held him fast. He swung more than three stories above the ground, feeling his stomach rise up into his throat.

"Don't get green on me, son," the general said as he was lowered beside Roy. "Close your eyes if you need to and think about the story."

Both lines were lowered. Roy kept his eyes open and watched as the floor got closer. This really wasn't so bad..."I liked when they were setting sail," Roy said. "And when Silver showed he trusted Jim Hawkins!"

"Pieces of eight!" Jenkins cried as he slid down beside them. He squawked just like Long John

Silver's parrot. "Pieces of eight!"

Roy laughed and before he knew it, he was on the ground. The harnesses came off quickly.

"I like you, Roy," the general said. "You've got an adventurer's heart!"

Roy's smiled, feeling good. He was ready.

Looking around, Roy saw that they had landed in the mall's food court. It was completely deserted. Tables were overturned. An ice cream stand had been ravaged. Bits of hot dogs, hamburgers, pizzas, and Chinese food were scattered everywhere.

"Looks like the monsters were here," said Jenkins.

"The question is, where did they go?" asked Roy.

"That's for you to discover," said the general.

The mall stretched out in three directions. Right, left, and dead ahead. Roy reached out with his power. The panic of the crowds flooding through the exits clouded his thoughts. He pushed it away and focused…Suddenly, he made contact!

"Three of them," Roy said. "Gecko, Gila, and Gopher." He pointed to the right arm of the mall. "They're in the big department store down this way."

"What about the other two?" the general asked. "The armadillo and the chuckwalla?"

"I'm not sure," Roy said. "But there are still people in the department store. A bunch."

"Then that's where we start," said the general.

CHAPTER 8

Amy still wasn't saying much when they reached Puget Sound. Everyone else cheered. Amy just looked sullen.

"Hey, smiley," Jean said. She shook Amy's knee. "Don't get all excited on my account or anything, but this means we've finished the first leg of the journey. Up north a ways, then past Port Angeles and Cape Flattery, and we'll hit the ocean."

"I'm, like, so thrilled," Amy said. She didn't even look up from her laptop computer. "Besides, it's gonna be *freezing* up there."

"Better than taking Godzilla to Seattle, don't you think?"

Amy looked up from her computer. An idea was forming in her mind.

The caravan stopped, and everyone watched as Godzilla and the other monsters splashed about in the much larger body of water. The river they'd been following was pretty narrow for creatures twenty-five stories high. Puget Sound was so wide they couldn't see the other side!

Amy used her power and leaped into Godzilla's mind. She let him know what the military had planned.

He didn't like the idea of the cold any better than she did.

Hiro approached. He seemed more relaxed than he had been before. "Okay, Amy," he said. "There are some boats on the approach. I need you to make sure Godzilla and his pals let them pass so they can pick us up."

"Okay," Amy said. She smiled, but didn't look up. "And you want me to get them to go up north, too. Where it's *freezing*." Amy looked over at him and batted her eyelashes. "They're not gonna like that too much. And *I'm* not thrilled, either."

"Oh, boy," Jean said under her breath.

Hiro frowned. "Amy, this is what we *need* to do. It's not a discussion."

"Oh!" Amy said. "I didn't realize it was an order. I guess you're gonna throw me in irons or something if I don't cooperate. Or send me home. I sup-

pose you guys can handle old Godzilla a lot better
than I can?"

Anger registered on Hiro's handsome face. But
only for a moment. He crammed it back down.
Then forced a smile. *"Amy..."*

"Here's the deal," Amy said. "If you're nice to me
again, then no problem. I'll take 'em north for you.
You might have to be extra *specially* nice, but—"

Hiro's smile broke. "Amy, this is ridiculous. I don't
know if you have a crush on me or what. If you do,
I'm sorry. I think the world of you. But you'd do better with someone your *own* age."

Jean cringed. "Wrong move, slick."

Amy's eyes narrowed. She coiled her power and
let it spring out.

In the water, Godzilla roared. He turned and led
the monsters south.

Amy looked back to her computer.

"Amy," Hiro said urgently. "This is unwise. There
are people—"

The twelve-year-old raised a single finger to
silence the scientist. "Like you said, Doctor...this
isn't a discussion."

Back at the mall, Roy, Jenkins, and the general
found Gecko in the bedding department. A group
of people were clustered in the corner. They
watched as the large lizard sped across the ceiling,

smashing the lights with his tail. Glass rained down and a woman screamed.

Gecko turned at the noise and made a loud *tick-tick-tick-tick-tick-tick* sound. His tongue flicked out at them.

The general reached for his weapon.

"No!" Roy said. "Gecko doesn't want to hurt anybody."

Gecko whipped his head around and went back to his work. The lizard was yellow, with brown bands crossing his fifteen-foot body and tail. The disks on his toes allowed him to cling to any surface.

Roy noticed the rest of what Gecko had been up to. The bedding department had been savaged. Mattresses were piled up in the center of the room, along with twisted bed frames.

"He wants to hibernate," Roy said. "In fact, he *should* be hibernating—it's that time of year for him. And he doesn't like the light. Or the heat outside."

"Yeah," Jenkins said. "We've got lizards like him up by my parents' house. They crawl under rocks or piles of stuff during the day."

The general nodded. Footsteps came from behind him. He turned to greet about a dozen SWAT team members and green-jacketed soldiers.

"Reporting for duty, sir!" said the ranking officer.

"Stay calm and we'll get through this," the general responded to the new arrivals. Then he gestured to the people who were afraid to leave their hastily made bunker at the back of the store.

"All right, you people," he called to the terrified civilians. "I want you to come toward us slowly. Stay near the outside walls at all times." He patted his weapon. "You'll be safe. We'll protect you if he tries anything."

Nearly two dozen people inched their way closer. They were nearly there when a cracking came from above—and the ceiling collapsed!

The people screamed and ran. A man fell and twisted his ankle. One of the SWAT members helped him get to safety.

Roy looked at the pile of debris in the center of the room. Gecko had fallen right into it, and he was thrashing around, flinging away bits of the ceiling that had clung to the suction cups on his toes.

A piece of plaster came sailing at Roy's head. The general yanked him out of the way. One of the soldiers was hit in the shoulder.

Someone started firing. The deafening roar of weapons filled the store. Yellow flame leaped from the muzzles of a half-dozen guns.

"No!" the general hollered. "Cease fire!"

When Roy looked back to the debris, he saw that Gecko had fled. He looked up at the hole in the ceiling.

"He's upstairs," Roy said. "With the other two. And they're *not* happy."

The general sighed. "This isn't going to be as easy as I'd hoped."

Roy followed the soldiers up the escalator to the second floor. He could *feel* how upset Gecko had become after the attack. And he understood. Somehow he had to calm Gecko and the others. Roy's big problem was trying to figure out how to reason with them.

It was the same problem he had with Amy. When an idea came into her head, she just acted on it, without thinking it through.

No, thought Roy, these monsters were actually worse than Amy. Far worse. She might be impulsive, even reckless, but at least he could reason with her some of the time. And she usually had some common sense.

In fact, he wished Amy was here right now. She'd know what to do. What *would* Amy do? he finally asked himself.

"General," Roy said a moment later.

The general looked over his shoulder. "Yes, son?"

They had reached the landing. The soldiers spread out. Most of the lights were out. There were no people here. Just them...and the monsters.

"Let me go talk to them," Roy said.

"Alone?"

Roy nodded.

"I can't let you do that."

"They're like little kids," Roy said. "If they see a bunch of people approaching, they're gonna get scared."

"I'll go with him," Jenkins said.

General Cutwell thought about it for a moment. Then he said, "All right. But you have to keep in visual range of the rest of us at all times. Deal?"

Roy nodded.

He closed his eyes and blanketed the entire floor of the department store with his power. He sensed their location: "Electronics."

Roy opened his eyes and went to the left. Jenkins was right behind him. The others kept a safe distance.

Gecko, Gila, and Gopher were playing with the big TVs. Nudging them. Batting them from one to the other, the way kids might play hot potato.

They froze when they saw Roy. Gecko rose up on straight, stiff legs.

Roy knew what that meant. He'd been on the Internet this morning, checking out sites about geckos and gilas and armadillos. Gecko was getting ready to attack!

CHAPTER

9

"Don't worry," Roy said. "No one's going to hurt you."

Behind him, he heard the SWAT leader start to unholster his weapon.

"*Don't,*" Roy said.

Jenkins stopped.

Roy knew what he had to do.

Ever since Mom and Dad had gone away, he'd tried to be a realist. He made fun of his sister for her wild dreams and her playful nature. But the truth of it was that he envied her. A lot. He was afraid to just let go and enjoy himself again. Afraid that the moment he let himself really be happy again, something would happen to ruin it all.

He couldn't be selfish like that anymore. Not with these guys depending on him. Roy thought about the happier times when he'd been little. Laughing and playing with Amy. Chasing her around the house. Surprise parties. Fun times with Mom and Dad.

And the games...all the games!

He gently eased his memories into the monsters' minds. Gecko relaxed and started hopping around.

"Hopscotch," Roy said. "That's right!"

He got Gopher and Gila playing leapfrog, then finally coaxed them all to play a game of hide-and-seek.

"Only it's Chuck and Armie who are hiding," said Roy. He put pictures of them in the minds of Gecko, Gopher, and Gila. "And we're the ones who have to seek!"

Gila came over and flipped Roy up onto his back. Roy laughed wildly as Jenkins climbed on, and together they rode with the other monsters onto the third floor of the mall. The soldiers had to run to catch up. The center section of the mall was hollow. Roy could look down from the third-floor railing and see people on the first floor.

Gila leaped down to the first floor, but he was slower-moving than the others. They found Chuck, the giant chuckwalla, in a ladies' clothing store. He'd gotten separated from the others, so he had puffed his lizard body up in order to wedge himself in for security.

Unfortunately, three women had been hiding in

the dressing rooms at the time. They were trapped. And if Chuck puffed himself up any more, they'd be crushed!

Roy had Gila approach Chuck and "tag" him with his forked tongue.

"You're it!" Roy cried. He used his power to make Chuck understand the rules of the game.

The chuckwalla let the air out of his massive lungs and waddled ahead, hoping to tag Gila in return. The women fled from the dressing rooms.

Roy was having the time of his life!

Armie, the giant armadillo, was down in the basement, digging a tunnel to who knows where. They coaxed him out.

Roy promised them plenty more fun and games. But first, they had to go back with the others. The monsters agreed. They left the mall with him. Gecko still had energy to burn, so they let him climb the mall's outside walls until he tired.

General Cutwell came to Roy and shook his hand. "Good job, lad!"

City officials blocked off the streets leading to the waterfront. Soon, Roy was sitting atop Gila as he led the monsters in a quickly organized parade. People lined up to see the spectacle. They laughed and cheered!

Roy thought about what the general had called him: an adventurer. He liked that! And this *was* an adventure. A wonderful adventure he would always remember.

If only Amy could be here with him!

Amy sat alone at the rear of one of the boats the army had sent. They were approaching Seattle. Amy had kept the monsters close enough to the shoreline to make Hiro and the others nervous.

She knew she was acting like a brat. But Hiro had hurt her feelings! And...and...

Amy's thoughts stopped there. She didn't know what to think, or do, next.

Jean Farady appeared. "Hey, boss."

"Hey."

"You wanna talk about it?"

Amy looked away for a long moment. Then she blurted, "He hates me."

"Hiro doesn't hate you," Jean reassured her. "He's just got a job to do, that's all. This little detour...it's not making things any easier, y'know."

"Good."

Jean looked surprised. "Okay. If that's how you really feel about it."

Amy shook her head. "I don't," she whispered.

"Then why don't you tell me what's *really* bothering you?"

"It's bad," Amy said in a low voice. "Stupid."

"I doubt that."

Amy studied her shoes. "Godzilla's got someplace to go. When this is over, *you've* got a place to go. So does Hiro. So does *everybody* here. Except me and Roy. All we've got is Crestview. And Billy was right. Running away sucks. I wouldn't even consider it. But...I just wish we had a home, too. That's all. Like I said, it's stupid. Just a stupid dream. Roy's right. All my dreams are stupid."

"Wow. You didn't have much on your mind, did you?"

Amy looked up. "I guess I'm being kind of selfish, right? I mean, I shouldn't be jealous of Godzilla. He's my friend."

"That's up to you, boss," Jean said. "I'm not here to judge you. I just thought you'd like some company."

Suddenly, Amy's powers kicked into overdrive. She leaped to her feet and saw the port of Seattle in the distance. Godzilla and the others had seen it, too. They had also seen something at one of the docks that was making them very upset.

"What's going on?" Amy asked.

Jean produced a pair of binoculars and handed them to Amy. She saw a large military ship at the dock. Roy was there. Along with General Cutwell. And all of the little guys, too. A crane was lifting them from the dock and lowering them into the ship's hold.

"That's the ship we'll be traveling on," said Jean. "It will take us to Godzilla's new island home."

Suddenly, Amy sensed something that made her afraid. "Godzilla," she whispered.

Amy and Jean turned to see Godzilla stomping toward the ship. Varan was at his side. The snakes were pouring on speed, leaping past them. Kamacuras flew overhead, holding Kumonga.

"No," Amy whispered. "They've got the wrong idea. Godzilla thinks something bad is happening to Gila, Gopher, and the others. All they see is a big silver beast, and they think it's swallowing up their little friends!"

A roar came from above. A pair of fighter jets swept in. They fired on the water in front of Godzilla as a warning.

But he kept coming.

Massive waves were kicked up. Small boats were overturned. People clung to one another and struggled to swim to shore.

The pier collapsed. The huge shopping plaza overlooking the water was torn from its moorings. It tipped over and sank while people swam to safety.

The celebration the people had been holding for Roy and the little guys had turned into a nightmare!

Amy had to do something.

The ridges along Godzilla's back were glowing

with blue-white fire. He was rearing back—as if to loose his flames upon the dock!

Amy saw the fighter jets swooping in again and knew she had only seconds to act. She looked at all the destruction and realized this had been her fault. If she hadn't been so childish and selfish, if she had listened to Hiro and Jean, Godzilla and the biggest monsters would never have come this close to civilization!

Enough, thought Amy. *I have to fix this!*

She pushed her power harder than ever before. Instantly, she was inside the mind of Gila, Gopher, and the other little monsters on the big ship.

They were terrified!

Quickly, she made Godzilla feel their fear—and understand that he was the cause of it. In the water, Godzilla stopped. The blue-white fire faded from his back.

Godzilla turned and went back to a deeper spot in the water. His friends joined him. The waves they'd caused settled.

The fighter jets flew over his head. Seeing Godzilla's retreat, the pilots held their fire.

Amy turned—and saw Hiro standing nearby. He sighed and nodded.

The danger was over.

CHAPTER 10

The big military ship safely shoved off, heading for the South Pacific. On board were Amy, Roy, Hiro, Jean, General Cutwell, and the smaller monsters.

Godzilla and the bigger monsters swam beside the ship. Kumonga, the giant spider, and Kamacuras, the giant praying mantis, were on a long steel barge that was being towed behind the ship.

After two weeks at sea, the island finally came into sight. White sandy beaches led to thick green jungles and rocky terrain that rose high into the blue sky.

"Land ho, ye bunch o' swabbies!" Roy hollered. He sounded like a pirate from one of his prized books.

Amy and Hiro laughed. They looked back at the rear deck of the ship and saw the smaller monsters peering excitedly toward shore. Even Gecko and Gila were out and about, though it was the middle of the day. Normally, they preferred the hold they shared with Gopher.

Godzilla was wading through the water, roaring with delight as he approached the island's white sand beach. Yellowback and Rattler were keeping clear of him because of the waves he kicked up.

Varan suddenly rose out of the water and leaped into the air!

"Whoa!" the general cried as he walked across the deck to Hiro. Together, they watched Varan fly to the island and disappear somewhere over its hills. The general shook his head. "Doctor, did you know he could do that? *Fly*, I mean?"

"Of course," Hiro said quickly. "It's in my report."

The general sighed.

Amy and Roy walked up to Hiro. A shadow fell over them. They looked up.

"Kamacuras and Kumonga!" Amy cried.

"Very good," said Hiro, pleased. During their journey, he had taught them the proper kaijuological names for these giant creatures.

Kamacuras was flying over them, carrying Kumonga. They buzzed by Godzilla on their way to the island. He shook his arms impatiently, then moved faster to reach the shore. The snakes worked hard to keep up.

Amy decided to tease Godzilla, too. She concentrated and tried to touch his mind.

But...she couldn't.

It felt as if a storm cloud had moved into her thoughts. A violent buzzing overcame her senses.

Amy pulled back.

Hiro looked at her strangely. "Are you all right?"

"I just tried to read Godzilla and something stopped me. I can't say exactly what it was, but it gave me the creeps."

Hiro called out to Roy, who was standing near the ship's rail, looking at the island with a pair of binoculars. He turned to Hiro with excitement.

"Is that what I think it is?" Roy asked. He pointed at a crest upon the island.

"Yes," Hiro said. "There's an inactive volcano at the center of this island. In fact, most islands in this region were *made* by volcanoes."

"Cool," Roy said. "Can we check it out? It would be so great if we could."

"Maybe. Do me a favor, would you? Use your psychic ability to see what's on Godzilla's mind."

Roy shrugged. "Sure."

He concentrated. Then, he jumped as if something had bitten him. "What the heck was *that*?"

Hiro shook his head. "That proves it. Something's up." He took Amy and Roy to the general.

"Maybe we should keep the little guys on the ship

until we have a chance to check it out ourselves,"
the general said after Hiro explained the problem.

"The *little* guys?" Roy asked. He smiled broadly.
"You mean Gila and the others?"

"I had a hamster once," the general said.
"Gopher there kinda reminds me of him. Even if he
is twenty feet taller."

"Let's go ashore," suggested Amy. "Maybe I'll
have better luck off the ship."

General Cutwell looked to Hiro. The scientist
nodded agreement, and the general lifted the radio
he carried and called Eddings, the communications
officer. "We're going ashore. Raise Dr. Mason for
us. Patch him through the second you have him.
Cutwell out."

Soon Hiro, General Cutwell, Amy, Roy, and a
handful of soldiers, including Jean, were trans-
ferred to a small powerboat. A mighty winch lowered it down into the water.

The general turned to Roy as they descended.
"How's your height thing doing? I know sometimes
you have a problem—"

"No big deal," Roy said. "*Now.*" He grinned ear
to ear. "I think your little push back at the mall
cured me for good."

The general laughed.

Amy eyed her twin brother. What was up with
him? He was never this way before, happy to rush

off into the unknown. She didn't know if she should be pleased about this change in him or not. She had always depended on him to be the level-headed one. From the ship, Amy heard a familiar *tick-tick-tick-tick-tick!*

She turned to see all five of the "little guys" looking down at her. Gecko was ticking like crazy. She had a feeling the younger monsters knew they were being left behind. It made them sad.

"We'll be back soon," she whispered. She only wished she believed it herself. Smiling, she waved at them.

The powerboat lurched as it connected with the water. Amy lost her balance, but a strong hand gripped her shoulder and steadied her. Amy looked up into the kind face of Jean Farady.

"Hey, boss, how ya doin'?" the blond-haired officer asked.

Amy smiled. "Why do you keep calling me boss?"

"I like the way you handle things, young lady. I'm proud to serve with you."

"Really?" Amy asked. Her whole face lit up.

"Really," Jean said.

Amy gave Jean a smile as the boat sped closer toward the island, where Godzilla was. In minutes, the boat was slowing. A small detail stayed with the boat as a standard precaution. Amy, Roy, Hiro, the general, and Jean waded to land.

The beach was lovely. Behind it was a thick wall of trees. Each tree had enormous green leaves with pointy tips.

Amy and Roy immediately attempted to make contact with Godzilla. Again they failed.

The general picked up his radio again. He shook his head. "I can't seem to raise Eddings on our transport ship. All I'm getting is static."

Amy looked around. Where were Dr. Mason and his crew? She wondered what was keeping the welcoming committee. In fact, that question seemed to be on everyone's mind as they stood on the deserted beach.

"We radioed Mason days ago," said the general. "Hiro, Jean, perhaps we should get the children to the boat, at least until we've established—"

Suddenly, a cry came from above. Everyone looked up to see Rodan sweep across the sky.

"Now this is more like it," the general said.

Amy disagreed. "I'm not so sure."

Suddenly, the ground began to tremble.

"Shock waves!" Hiro yelled. "It's Rodan, he's making shock waves! Everyone take cov—"

There was no time for him to finish. Rodan's wings made supersonic shock waves that hit the ground like invisible fists, kicking up walls of sand.

Amy, Roy, and the others were blown backward. They spun and rolled for twenty feet before coming

to a stop. Even Godzilla lost his balance a moment and was nearly torn from his feet.

Finally, Amy and the others rose. They looked behind them and were alarmed to see dozens of trees snapped in half by the waves of force.

"Why is he attacking?" Amy asked Hiro.

The scientist shook his head. "I don't know."

High above, Rodan soared back in their direction once more. He targeted Godzilla alone with his next set of shock waves. Godzilla turned his face from the force. When he looked back, Rodan was on him, pecking at Godzilla with his strong beak, then slapping at him with his claws.

"We've got to get back to the boat," the general said.

"No chance," Hiro said. "Look!"

He pointed at the boat. The shock waves had spun it end over end, back into the water. It was sinking. The soldiers lay strewn across the beach, unconscious.

Behind Amy, another thundering sounded. A dozen trees collapsed with a sharp crack, and the second monster who lived on this island appeared.

Anguirus charged right at them!

CHAPTER

II

Anguirus was a mutant dinosaur, an Ankylosaurus who had been exposed to radiation, like Godzilla, and become a giant monster.

He was sixty meters tall, with many sharp spikes.

"Run!" the general shouted as the monster raced toward them on four legs. The general drew his sidearm and aimed it at the huge creature.

Jean pulled her weapon and stood at his side. "Go! We'll distract him so you can get away!"

"No," Amy said. She knew her friends would never survive against Anguirus.

Hiro grabbed her hand and nearly yanked her off her feet.

"Look!" he said, pointing high. "There's a path just beyond those trees. It leads to higher ground."

Suddenly, a half-dozen figures dressed in camouflage fatigues appeared on that path. They were heavily armed.

"General!" Roy cried.

Cutwell and Jean spun to face the newcomers. A pair of sharp hisses sliced through the air. The general and his officer crumpled to the ground.

"Jean!" Amy cried. Then she saw it: Tiny darts jutted from her neck and the general's, too.

Amy and the others heard the thundering footfalls of Anguirus. Amy tried to use her power on the monster, but nothing happened.

She spun around. The armed men had cut off their retreat. They had no place to go!

Godzilla rose up and shrugged off Rodan. He saw the danger Amy was in. Anguirus was charging right for her!

Godzilla leaped high into the air. He brought his feet down *hard*, and the ground shook. Anguirus was thrown from his feet, his charge defeated.

Amy and the others were hurled into the air, too! They landed, rolling into crumpled heaps, unconscious.

Godzilla waited for several long moments, but his friends didn't move again. The behemoth was stunned. He'd tried to save Amy. To help her. But now...Godzilla tilted his head back and roared in anguish. His friends were hurt!

Then he felt it. A dark cloud swept into his thoughts. It crackled with terrible energy. It reminded Godzilla of the unnatural energies that had changed him from a dinosaur into a dinosaur-monster!

And along with the dark energies came *urges*. He felt a desire to go back to sea and find the silver ship that the girl and the smaller monsters had been riding upon. To find it—and smash it!

Godzilla fought the urges within him. They weren't *his* desires. Something else was trying to get inside his mind. Only this wasn't like the bright-faced girl. He had liked her. This energy was dark. And it wanted Godzilla to do what it said.

But Godzilla wouldn't. He roared in defiance!

From behind, Godzilla heard a splashing. He turned to see Yellowback and Rattler wash up on shore. They were twisting frantically. Godzilla wondered if they, too, were grappling with an invader inside their heads.

He looked down, hoping to see Amy and his other friends back on their feet. But something was moving his way.

The armored dinosaur!

Godzilla stepped to one side and let Anguirus tear past him. With a growl, Godzilla kicked the dinosaur hard enough to send him flying out into the water. Then he blasted him with his atomic flame, turning the water around him into steam!

Anguirus's eyes blazed with fury. He rammed into Godzilla's legs and knocked him to the ground.

With a savage cry, Anguirus flipped himself backward, digging the sharp spikes of his back into Godzilla's belly. Godzilla howled in pain and rage. He tried to shove his opponent away, but Anguirus wriggled, and all Godzilla could do was cry out.

Suddenly, a shadow rose up over them. Rattler!

The snake bit Anguirus on his unprotected underbelly and dragged him off Godzilla. Then Rattler whipped Anguirus back and forth a few times and hurled him away.

Godzilla used his tail to rise to his feet. He looked at Rattler in surprise. The snake had always fought him in the past. But now Rattler was *helping* him! Godzilla wondered why.

The dark crackling cloud pushed itself into Godzilla's mind once more, and then he *knew*. Rattler was fighting with Godzilla because they had the same enemy. Rattler was battling the dark cloud, too. And his will was strong—like Godzilla's!

A padding came from behind Godzilla. He looked down and saw Anguirus wobbling as he put his head down and tried to charge once again. Godzilla picked the dinosaur up and tossed him away with all his strength. Anguirus sailed through the air and disappeared in the distant jungle.

A buzzing captured Godzilla's attention. He saw Kamacuras flying overhead, carrying Kumonga. The duo flew toward the large silver ship floating on the water in the distance.

A moment later, Godzilla saw Kumonga drop down onto the silver ship's flat surface and start to tear. The mantis ripped off pieces with its pincer-like arms.

Godzilla turned from the sight. He knew it was the dark cloud making them do this. The same dark cloud that was trying to control him and drive him to hurt and destroy his friends.

But Godzilla would not listen to this cloud. He would fight it! Closing his eyes, Godzilla sniffed the air. He felt the dark pull of the cloud. It came from the direction of the volcano in the distance.

Godzilla set off to find the cloud. And when he found it, he'd make it pay!

Amy slowly stirred. She saw Roy lying nearby on the beach, and she quickly sat upright.

"Roy!" she cried. "Roy, are you—"

He moaned and started to come around. Hiro was off to one side of him. He was also rising.

The men in the camouflage fatigues with the guns were scattered behind them. None of them were moving. Hiro immediately disarmed them. Then he nodded toward the shore.

Rodan was stuck with his head in the sand. He looked like an ostrich! It would have been funny, except—

He was breaking *free!*

Amy went to Jean and the general. They were still out cold. She heard a rumbling. Felt a familiar anger sear her mind. *Godzilla!*

He was moving toward the volcano at the center of the island. Rattler was at his side.

Amy tried to leap into Godzilla's thoughts, but the crackling black cloud forced her away. Still...she *had* been able to feel his anger, and that was more than she'd been able to do before.

Varan appeared on the horizon, flying toward the behemoth. Godzilla roared with an out-of-control rage and loosed his atomic flame. Varan was sent veering off course.

Hiro put his hand on Amy's shoulder. He nodded to the rise where the armed men had appeared. "We have to get out of here."

Amy looked back at Jean and the general. "But we can't just leave them."

Hiro nodded. One at a time, he dragged the unconscious pair to safety, hiding them off to one side of the rise. He placed all of the confiscated weapons with them.

A sharp cry came from the beach. Amy saw Rodan finally free himself. She was worried he would fly their way. Instead, he shook the sand off, then leaped into the air toward Godzilla.

Behind Amy, one of the men in camouflage fatigues started groaning.

"Amy," Hiro said, "it would help us to know what's going on here. That man waking up—"

She understood at once. Her power didn't work properly on the monsters. But maybe she could try it on this soldier. Amy closed her eyes. Her brow furrowed. "Oh, *that's* interesting," she whispered.

The man sat up. He still looked groggy.

"Go to sleep," Amy said crossly.

The man's body jerked once and he fell back, unconscious.

"Whoa," Roy said, eyes wide. "I didn't know you could do *that*. You knocked him out just by thinking about it."

"I think it helped that I was really, really mad."

"Amy, what did you discover from reading his thoughts?" Hiro asked.

"That man you told us about? Dr. Mason? He made a deal with these terrorists. That's who these guys are." Amy gestured to the unconscious men in the camouflage fatigues. "Dr. Mason had discovered a way to communicate with Rodan and Anguirus. He used an energy beam of some kind to do it. But he needed money, so he made a deal with these terrorists to turn Rodan and Anguirus—"

"He made them into living weapons," Hiro finished for her.

"Right," Amy said.

"We'll have to shut down Mason's control center," Hiro said.

"It's in the middle of the mountain," Amy said. "I saw it in that soldier's mind. They've got guards and metal doors with sensors all around."

Hiro frowned. "I wonder what Mason's using to power all of this?"

"I don't know, but I've got to try to reach Godzilla's mind. I've got to find a way to warn him," Amy said.

"But how can you?" Roy asked. "You couldn't get through to him before. I couldn't, either."

"Neither of us could do it alone," said Amy softly. "But..."

She held out her hand to her brother.

Roy nodded. He took his sister's hand and held it tightly. Hiro watched as the twins closed their eyes and tried to reach Godzilla together.

CHAPTER

12

Godzilla and Rattler were only a few paces from the volcano when Rodan attacked.

Flapping his wings, Rodan created shock waves that sent Rattler whipping about.

Godzilla anchored himself. He ignored the raging wind and the terrible howls. Rodan came close and Godzilla batted him with one claw. The flier fell to the earth, and Rattler pounced on him.

Now it was Varan's turn to attack Godzilla.

Godzilla was in no mood. He wrestled with the lizard monster, then tossed him against the volcano. The impact shook the entire island and made swarms of two-leggers run screaming from the volcano.

Godzilla considered squashing the two-leggers. But the crackling black cloud was still in his head, fighting for control. And he began to wonder—

Was it really so bad what the cloud wanted him to do? Smash the silver box on the water? Bring down the places where the two-leggers lived, across the ocean?

Was that *really* so bad?

He almost didn't care anymore. The bright-faced girl was gone from his mind. All he wanted to do now was vent his anger.

Nothing else mattered.

No one else mattered!

It was then he felt something familiar in his head...something warm...a shining presence.

It was the bright-faced girl! She was all right! And her brother was with her, too!

Godzilla's mind began to see all that Amy and her brother had been through. All that they had learned. Roy had been hurt. And so he'd shut himself off from others so that he couldn't be hurt again.

Amy had been hurt, too. When her parents died, she had decided to place her desires and whims above everything else, believing no one else would ever care about her needs. But putting her whims above all else had resulted in chaos. Destruction. Rash and selfish action without care.

Godzilla felt that way about his anger. Nothing else mattered...no one mattered. But no. That might have been true once, because he had been hurt.

Badly hurt, like Roy. And he'd felt alone, like Amy.

But he had learned. Just as Amy and Roy had learned. There were more important things than what he wanted, what he desired.

Godzilla thought of the other monsters. The little monsters. His friends. And he thought of the other two-leggers who were still on that ship.

He had the power to stop the attack on the ship. With a roar, Godzilla turned away from the volcano and started back to the shore.

He would help his friends, no matter what the dark cloud in his head told him to do!

Amy and Roy sank to their knees. Breaking through the beam's power to reach Godzilla had exhausted them.

Amy looked up to see Godzilla heading out into the water. Rodan followed, though Rattler was hanging onto his wing. The pterosaur awkwardly zigged and zagged through the air. The constantly shifting weight of his unwelcome passenger threw him off. No matter what Rodan tried, he couldn't shake Rattler free!

A rustling came. It was followed by heavy, inhuman footfalls. Had Anguirus returned?

A dark green snout poked out from between a pair of trees. A bulky form waddled closer, and the trees *snapped.*

"Gila!" Roy cried.

The other smaller monsters were right behind. They were all soaking wet.

"Be careful," Hiro urged.

Roy reached out with his power. "It's okay! I can communicate with them."

"Really? Hmm. It must be because they're young," Hiro mused. "Their minds aren't fully developed, so the beam isn't affecting them."

"They got scared when Kamacuras and Kumonga attacked the carrier," Roy said. He patted Chuck's flank. "So they swam for the island, looking for us!"

Amy heard sounds. "We have to leave. More of Mason's guys are coming. I can hear them."

Gopher and Armie bounced in place. Gecko made a happy *tick-tick-tick-tick-tick.*

"What's with them?" Amy asked.

Roy grinned. "They're wondering if it's time for all those fun and games I promised them."

Hiro raised a single eyebrow. "As a matter of fact, I think it just might be. In any case, it's time to take the battle to Dr. Mason."

He pointed at the volcano.

The group was soon standing near one of the volcano's entrances.

"I don't see any guards," Roy said.

Hiro nodded. "They may have fled. Or they could be on the beaches, watching the ship."

Amy jumped as steam hissed out of a crack in the earth next to her. "What is *that?*" Amy asked.

"The volcano venting its heat," Hiro said.

A sound came from above. A helicopter filled with terrorists!

Gecko became upset and he began to tick. He turned in the other direction and rose up on straight legs, ready to spring at an enemy.

"What is it?" Roy asked the monster. Gecko wasn't looking in the direction of the helicopter at all. He was looking the other way.

A hiss came and Yellowback appeared, winding his way through a pair of boulders above. Geckos and snakes were natural enemies!

"Run!" Hiro said.

Amy and Roy didn't need any urging. Pops came as dart guns fired at them.

Then a door opened in front of them and a half-dozen more terrorists appeared. It had been a trap!

A sharp, terrible cracking sounded from beneath Amy's feet. She gasped as fissures opened all around them.

"It can't take the weight of all of us!" Hiro said.

The ground beneath them shattered, and the entire group plunged into darkness!

CHAPTER

13

Amy screamed as they fell. Steam hissed up to greet them. She landed on a hard surface. The others crashed down beside her. Rock and loose earth closed in from above. She was covered in the stuff!

For a moment, Amy was terrified that they were going to be buried beneath all the debris. She couldn't see the sun anymore.

The rain of earth and stone ended. She sat up, brushing off little rocks.

"Roy? Hiro?" she asked.

Movement came from all around her.

"We're here," Hiro said.

"Blech!" Roy muttered. "I think I swallowed some of this stuff!"

Amy giggled. She couldn't help herself.

"Fine. You laugh," Roy groused. He shook his head. And *smiled.* "Actually, it *is* pretty funny, isn't it?"

A light suddenly flared. Hiro had taken a small flashlight from his jacket. He shined it all around. All five of the little guys were there. Their backs had formed a temporary roof, keeping Hiro and the others from being crushed.

Some of the monsters were getting snug. They liked it here, buried deep within the earth. Time to hibernate.

"None of that!" Hiro said. "We've got work to do." He turned to Roy. "We've got some air, but I don't know how long it will last. Armie and Gopher need to dig us a way out of here while the other guys hold up the roof."

Roy nodded. He used his power, appealing to Armie and Gopher's curiosity.

Actually, they *did* want to know what else might be down here. They started digging. Armie and Gopher worked side by side, tossing rock and debris to Gopher's right and Armie's left. That way, the others could walk behind them without worrying about being hit by rocks or handfuls of loosely packed earth.

"Is it just me, or is it getting hotter?" Amy asked after a time. "What if they're taking us right into the heart of the volcano?"

Roy shook his head. "No way. Gopher and Armie have good instincts. They sense something tasty up ahead."

Suddenly, rock and stone gave way to steel and concrete. Gopher busted through a heavy wall, and artificial light burst in their faces.

The monsters happily plunged forward. They bit into huge bags of fruit and meat.

It was a supply depot!

"Let me go first," Hiro said. He went up between the giant monsters, patting their flanks, and poked his head through the opening. He came to a door and carefully peeked out.

"I see some kind of corridor," Hiro said. "It's not wide enough for the little guys. They'll have to stay here."

Roy gestured at the little monsters. They were busily munching away on sixty-pound bags of sugar and other supplies. "I don't think it's gonna be a problem."

"Heat suits," Hiro said. He pointed at a row of silver suits with black visors. "I think I can guess what Mason's been up to now. Amy, Roy—each of you put one of these on. We should be able to reach the control center from here."

They put them on. As they went into the hall, the little guys became sad once again.

"We'll be right back for you," Amy promised.

"You fellas be good, okay?"

The monsters shuffled in place.

Roy sent a message into their heads. *More fun and games if you're good!*

They understood that one and happily wagged tails and made glad ticking sounds.

Hiro led Amy and Roy down the long gray corridor. There were no cameras or sensors here. And it *was* hot. Very hot. But with the heat suits, the trio was able to walk down the series of corridors.

"It's getting hotter," Amy said.

"Then we must be close."

They passed through a door and entered a large darkened area. At first, all they could see was a ledge with a guardrail. Beyond it was some odd flickering yellow and red light from below. They could hear raised voices. Activity.

"Come on," Hiro said.

The ledge made a full circle around an area three hundred feet across. The heat was almost unbearable, even with the suits.

"Mason always did like it hot," Hiro muttered.

They came to the ledge's guardrail and looked down. Amy and Roy were startled to see several round man-made platforms below. On them were banks of huge machines with people zipping about from work station to work station. Everyone wore heat suits.

The reason lay far below.

"The volcano," Amy said with a gasp. She looked down into a swirling sea of lava that was the heart of the volcano.

"Mason's brought the volcano back to life," Hiro said. "He's using it as a power source. He actually thinks he can control it!"

Amy noticed several large viewing screens below. On one of the screens, Godzilla was in deep water, fighting Kamacuras, Kumonga, Varan, and Rodan. Rattler was still fighting at his side. The ship had sustained a lot of damage, but it was still afloat.

Godzilla punched the giant bulbous head of the spider, Kumonga. He bathed Kamacuras with his atomic flame. Rattler had wrapped his body around Varan and was squeezing hard. Rodan circled overhead, looking for an opening.

"I don't understand this!" a man in a crimson heat suit wailed. "What's making them fight? They should all be under by now!"

"Mason," Hiro whispered.

A terrorist in a white heat suit approached. "Dr. Mason, we've rounded up all the soldiers from the beach. They're unharmed, as you've instructed."

"Good. We're going to need as many human subjects as we can get," Mason said. He tilted his visor back so that his hawklike features could be seen.

Amy felt herself becoming angry. *Human* subjects? Mason wanted to control people next? She had to stop this. And she thought she knew just how to do it, too.

But she stopped herself, realizing she shouldn't rush into something like this on her own. Instead, she reached out with her power and described her plan to Hiro and Roy.

"Sounds good," Hiro said. "But don't start with Mason. I have some other ideas for him."

"I can help," Roy added.

Amy concentrated—and the man who'd been speaking to Mason stiffened. Then he unholstered his weapon and used its stock to smash all the video monitors!

"What—what—what—" Mason sputtered. "Are you insane? What are you doing?"

Mason was so intent on the soldier's actions that he didn't notice what the technician next to him was doing. The man typed in a series of codes that Amy was giving him—with Hiro's help. And in seconds the room went black.

"What's happening here?" Mason hollered.

The three figures standing above knew, but they were too busy to speak with the misguided scientist.

Mason ran about, desperately attempting to restore his systems. He didn't even notice the trembling footsteps and the terrible roars from without.

But his people noticed. They hollered and ran from the control room in terror.

Then a scraping noise came from above—and the roof was peeled away. Bright sunlight burst into the chamber and Godzilla looked down. He roared and even Mason trembled.

The leader of the terrorists yanked out his radio as he ran from the room. "Abort! Mission abort! I want a full evacuation! Everyone get off this island—now!"

Kamacuras and Kumonga appeared at the lip of the volcano above, peering down. Varan was there. Yellowback and Rattler, too. Even Rodan circled angrily above.

Mason ignored them. He frantically pounded the keys. His machines roared back to life!

"Give it up," Hiro said at last.

Mason looked up at him.

Hiro raised his visor, despite the heat. He wanted Mason to know who had beaten him.

"So that's how you got Godzilla to come here," Mason said. He gestured at Amy and Roy. "The children have psychic powers! That's what those readings were!"

Godzilla roared again.

Mason went back to his keyboard. "Well, your friend up there can't harm my machines without hurting you, too! And by the time you can get down here, I'll have the system back on line. There are direct transmitters in the walls that don't depend on the satellite. Even Godzilla and his strong-willed friends won't be able to resist!"

Amy reached out with her power. She thought she could control Mason as she had the others. But she was hurled back by the force of Mason's mind. "The cloud. The lightning. All of it was coming from *him!*"

A crashing made everyone jump as Mason pounded on the keys. Gopher and Armie burst through the wall. The others followed. The little guys were about to start wrecking the equipment when Mason keyed in a final sequence. The machines sprang to life. And the swirling flow of lava far beneath turned yellow as the sun!

The little guys froze in fear as the small platforms started to collapse under their weight. Godzilla and the other monsters moaned and beat at the rim of the volcano far above. But Mason's machine was already gaining control over them.

"No!" Amy cried. She took Roy's hand. "Remember the dream? Godzilla's dream of how things could be? We have to make him remember it. We have to make them all understand!"

Roy nodded. He closed his eyes. With all the strength they had inside them, the twins focused their power and sent the blissful dream of home back into the minds of the monsters.

Hiro and Mason looked around. The walls appeared to melt away. Water rose all around them. The river from Godzilla's *dream*. They were seeing it as if it was real!

Mason grabbed a weapon one of the terrorists had dropped. He aimed it at the trio he could only barely make out above, but before he could fire, the door beside him burst open. General Cutwell and Jean Farady burst in. Both carried dart guns.

"I don't think so!" Jean shouted. A single hiss rang out and Mason fell against his keyboard, a dart jutting from his neck.

With a wicked smile, Mason reached out and struck a pair of keys on the computer board before sinking down. The general grabbed him and carted him from the room. Jean whistled to the little monsters, and they fled the way they'd come.

The images from Godzilla's dream started fading.

"What's happening?" Hiro asked.

"The machines," Amy said desperately. "They're getting stronger. Using more and more energy!"

Hiro looked down in horror at the swirling volcanic river far beneath them. The lava was rising. Fists of flame soared at them!

Rodan flew inside the mouth of the volcano and struck out with his shock waves. The banks of machines fell, some crashing through the floor into the molten river below. But the effects they had put into motion didn't stop.

"It's like Mason wanted to drive them crazy!" Roy said.

Godzilla started tearing at the walls of the volcano. Kumonga and Kamacuras attacked Varan.

And inside the volcano, Rodan shook the place apart.

"Remember the dream," Amy said. She used her power one last time. "It can still happen—you just have to want it bad enough!"

She funneled all her feelings of loneliness, all of her need as an orphan to have a place to call her own, a real home. And she poured it into Godzilla.

The behemoth was roaring, tilting his head back, about to release his flame on the inside of the volcano...

But he stopped.

Amy could feel him slowly regaining control of his anger. He looked to the other monsters, who had stopped their fighting. Rodan gave a great final caw and flew out of the volcano.

Jean entered the observation ledge from behind Amy. She put her hand on the twelve-year-old's shoulder. "Nice job, boss."

Amy was too exhausted to do anything but smile.

EPILOGUE

It was late in the day and the sun was setting. Amy and Roy sat on the beach. A nice breeze blew in from the east. Godzilla and the others were playing in the distance.

Jean Farady came up to the twins and crouched before them. "Well, that's it. Mason and the last of his friends are gone. How are you guys doing?"

Amy sighed. "It's been a busy day."

"I hear that. Look, I'm gonna get right to the point. I was just on the phone with my husband. We were wondering if you and Roy would like to stay with us for a while."

"You're married?" Amy said. She'd never even noticed the ring on her finger.

"Yes, I am. So—you two need time to think it over?"

Amy looked at Roy nervously.

Jean laughed. "I know what you two must be thinking—and I'm not even psychic. But I'll tell you, this has nothing to do with feeling sorry for the two of you guys. It's got a lot more to do with feeling sorry for Ben and me if you two say no. So—"

"We'd love it!" Roy said.

Amy laughed and gave her brother the biggest hug of their lives. Godzilla wasn't the only one who'd found a new home!

While on the shore, Hiro watched the monsters. General Cutwell came up to him.

"Something occurred to me," the general said. "This place doesn't have a name."

Hiro smiled. He looked off at Godzilla and the others. And closer still, the little guys playing hide-and-seek.

"It does now, General. Monster Island. You're standing on *Monster Island!*"

Far above, Rodan cried out with delight. Godzilla roared in agreement. And all the other monsters joined in.

It sounded as if they approved.

Read all of the books in the
Random House series!

Ask for these titles wherever books are sold.

OR

You .... der.

Ther .... one

Pleas .... rder.

❑ God...
  by S.. ...$3.99

❑ God...
  by S.. ...$3.99

❑ God...
  by S.. ...$3.99

❑ God...
  by S.. ...$3.99

❑ God...
  A Go.. *included!*
  (0-67.. .$11.99

❑ *The* ....
  The c.. *er*
  200 ....
  (0-67.. .$16.00

  Pric.. nly.
  All .... ery.